A Puzzle of Paws

To Marmite—our coal-black girlie with attitude.

GROSSET & DUNLAP
Published by the Penguin Group
Penguin Group (USA) LLC, 375 Hudson Street, New York, New York 10014, USA

USA | Canada | UK | Ireland | Australia | New Zealand | India | South Africa | China

penguin.com
A Penguin Random House Company

Text copyright © 2007, 2014 Sue Bentley. Illustrations copyright © 2007 Angela Swan. Cover illustration copyright © 2007 Andrew Farley. All rights reserved. First printed in Great Britain in 2007 by Penguin Books Ltd. First published in the United States in 2014 by Grosset & Dunlap, a division of Penguin Young Readers Group, 345 Hudson Street, New York, New York 10014. GROSSET & DUNLAP is a trademark of Penguin Group (USA) LLC. Printed in the USA.

Library of Congress Cataloging-in-Publication Data is available.

ISBN 978-0-448-46795-5   10 9 8 7 6 5 4 3 2 1

Magic Kitten

A Puzzle of Paws

SUE BENTLEY

Illustrated by Angela Swan

Grosset & Dunlap
An Imprint of Penguin Group (USA) LLC

★ Prologue ★

As a terrifying roar rang out, the young white lion froze. He should have known it was dangerous to come back home. He needed to find a safe hiding place.

Flame's thick white fur ignited with sparks, and there was a bright white flash. Where he had stood now crouched a tiny, long-haired, jet-black kitten. Above him an enormous menacing shape was outlined against the orange, pink, and red of the evening sky.

"Uncle Ebony!" Flame gasped.

Trembling with fear, he edged backward and crawled into a deep crack in a rock out of sight of his uncle.

There was a thud and a deep, rumbling growl as a heavy animal landed close to where the black kitten was hiding. Flame's tiny heart missed a beat. This was it! He was about to be dragged from his hiding place and taken prisoner—or worse.

Flame shrank against the cold stone, making himself as small as possible. As a shadow fell over the rocks, he bit back a soft whine of fear.

"Prince Flame? Do not be afraid. I

will protect you," a voice softly growled, and a kindly face with a scarred gray muzzle peered into the deep crack.

"Cirrus. I am glad to see you again!" Flame crawled out toward the old lion.

"But I do not think that even you can protect me from my uncle. He will do anything to keep the throne he stole from me."

Cirrus reached out a huge paw that was as big as Flame was now and drew the tiny kitten's body close. "The Lion Throne is rightfully yours, Prince Flame. One day you will take it back and free this land from evil."

Flame's bright emerald eyes flashed. "Let that day be now! I will face Ebony and fight him."

Cirrus narrowed his eyes and gave
a fond smile that showed worn yellow
teeth. "Bravely said. But first you must
grow strong and wise. Go from here. Use
this disguise and hide in the other world.
Return when the time is right."

Suddenly another deafening roar rang
out, and there came the sound of ironhard
claws scrabbling over rock. "Come out,
Flame, and let us finish this!" Ebony
roared.

"Go now, Prince," Cirrus urged. "Save
yourself. Go . . ."

Flame's long silky black fur began to
glow with sparks. He whined softly as he
felt the power building inside him and felt
himself falling. Falling . . .

Chapter
ONE

Rosie Swales hummed to herself
as she put food and clean water in her
gerbils' cage. "I love weekends. Yay! No
school!" she sang out.

"I thought you really liked school,"
said Jade, lying on her tummy on Rosie's
fake-fur rug. Jade lived next door and was
Rosie's best friend.

"I do. But I love spending time with

my animals even more!" Rosie replied, grinning. She had a huge attic bedroom, with a deep alcove. Shelves held various cages and glass tanks, and underneath them there was a large open-fronted wire pen for Daisy, Rosie's pet rabbit.

Rosie went to another cage. "Here you are, girls, have a peanut. Yum, yum. Is that tasty?"

Jade pulled a face. "Duh! As if those dumb rats are going to answer you!"

"Hey! You'll hurt Midge's and Podge's feelings! Besides, everyone knows that rats are very intelligent," Rosie said indignantly.

"Says you!" Jade scoffed. She opened a magazine and began flipping the pages. "You've got more animals in here than a pet store!"

"I know!" Rosie said, grinning. "If I'm going to work with animals when I grow up, I have to know all about them, don't I?"

She had started off with two pet rats and a hamster. Then she'd adopted Daisy the rabbit and some gerbils. Then some stick bugs and a tank of fish had needed a home. And just recently, two

parakeets had ended up staying with her
after their owner had to move away.

Jade rolled her eyes. "I swear that you
like animals better than people."

"Maybe I do like them better than
some people!" Rosie's eyes twinkled with
mischief. She leaped on Jade and started
tickling her.

Jade squealed with laughter and tried
to squirm away. "Stop it! Get off!" she
begged.

"Wimp!" Rosie crowed, wiggling her
fingers into her best friend's ribs.

Gasping for breath, Jade managed to
roll free. She sat up and tucked her dark
brown hair behind her ears. "I'd better
go now," she said when she'd stopped
laughing. "I told Mom I wouldn't stay
too long. Do you want to come with me?

I've got a great new game we can play."

Rosie felt really tempted, but then she remembered that she had lots of things to do. "No, I'd better not," she decided reluctantly. "I have to clean out my fish tank and pick some leaves for the stick bugs, and I really should clean Daisy's pen—"

"Whatever!" Jade interrupted. She did a pretend yawn.

"Sorry!" Rosie said, hoping that Jade

wasn't too disappointed. "I'll come over as soon as I've done all my pet chores."

"See you the day after tomorrow then. Too bad I don't have a fur coat and a long tail!" Jade said.

Rosie bit her lip, not sure what to say.

"I'm joking, silly!" Jade rolled up her magazine and swatted Rosie playfully on the shoulder. "Are you walking me to the door or what?"

"Of course I am!" Rosie jumped up and then linked arms with Jade as they went downstairs. At the front door, she stood and waved as Jade went through the front gate. "See you!"

"Later!" Jade called back over her shoulder.

As Rosie came back into the hall, her mom popped her head around the kitchen door. "Could you come in here a minute, dear? Your dad and I have something to tell you."

"Okay," Rosie said, going to sit next to her dad, who was at the table with a cup of coffee and a newspaper. "What is it, Dad?"

Mr. Swales looked up and smiled. "Good news. We just found the perfect house to move to."

"You're going to love it, too," Mrs. Swales said, spooning hot-chocolate mix into two mugs. She finished making the drinks and handed one to Rosie as she came and sat at the table.

"Thanks." Rosie took a sip of her hot chocolate, trying to ignore the sinking feeling in her tummy at the thought of moving.

Mr. Swales reached across to ruffle his daughter's short brown hair. "You do understand that we can't afford to live in this big house anymore, don't you?" he said gently.

Rosie stared into her cup and nodded miserably. "It's because you had to change jobs. Where's this new house?

Is it far away? Will I have to change schools and make new friends and—"

"Hold your horses!" her dad said, smiling. "It's just across town, on Milton Street. So you'll be able to go to the same school and see all your friends."

"Really?" Rosie leaped up and did a triumphant little dance around the kitchen. "That's great! I was dreading moving away, but everything's going to be all right now!"

Mr. and Mrs. Swales exchanged worried glances.

Rosie stopped jumping around. "What's wrong?"

"There's just one problem," her dad said. "The rooms in the new house are a lot smaller than here, especially the bedrooms. So I'm afraid there's not going to be any room for the pets."

"Oh." Rosie thought about this. "I'll miss having them all so close to me, but it won't be so bad if they have to live downstairs," she said.

"I don't think you understand, honey," her mom said calmly. "We're not going to have any room *at all* for all those cages and pens. Your dad and I have thought hard about this, and we've decided that you can keep Daisy, but you'll have to find new homes for all your other pets."

Rosie was stunned. She stared at her parents in disbelief. "You can't mean it!"

"I'm sorry, but there's no way around this," her dad said, looking uncomfortable.

"Rosie. You're going to have to try to be very grown-up about this. We all have to make sacrifices," her mom said gently.

A hot, hard feeling rose in Rosie's chest. "Well, I don't see why my pets should make any sacrifices. It's not their fault that we have to move!" She ran out of the kitchen, tears pricking her eyes.

"Rosie, wait!" her dad called.

As Rosie hurtled up the stairs two at a time, her mom's voice floated out after her. "She just needs time to get used to the idea—"

"I won't ever, ever get used to it! Not in a hundred million years!" Rosie said through gritted teeth as she went into her bedroom, slammed the door, and flung herself facedown onto her bed.

Chapter
TWO

"It's not fair! Why does this have to happen to me?" Rosie said miserably. She sat up against her pillows, stroking Daisy's long velvety ears. The rabbit was bigger than most fully grown cats and very beautiful, with soft gray fur and big brown eyes.

There was a scuffling noise from the rats' cage, where they were playing with a cardboard tube. Rosie felt a pang as she watched them playing happily. "Don't worry, you two. There's no way I'm going to let anyone take you away from me. And the same goes for the rest of you guys!" she promised, looking sadly at her other pets.

Leaving Daisy snuggled up on the quilt, Rosie got up and went over to the

fish tank. She removed the cover and
then used a tiny net to scoop out fish
droppings and any uneaten food. It
didn't take long, and the tank was soon
spick-and-span.

"Oh!" Rosie gasped.

She froze with disbelief.

There was something thrashing
around in the tank. Rosie crept forward
slowly, put her face close to the glass,
and saw that it was a tiny, long-haired,
black kitten! Its paws were skidding
on the tank's smooth glass sides as it
struggled to keep its head above water.

"Oh my goodness. You'll drown in
there!" She quickly reached in, grasped
the kitten, and hauled it to safety.

Rosie held the soaked little form
against her chest. The kitten's heart

was beating fast against her hand as it coughed and spit water.

"It's okay. You're safe now," she crooned. Grabbing a clean T-shirt that was lying on a chair, she wrapped it around the shivering kitten and gently began patting it. "I'll get you warm and dry."

"Thank you. I am feeling much better already," a tiny voice mewed.

Rosie's head shot up and she looked around the room in surprise. "Who's there? Who said that?"

Rosie felt a little paw tap at her chest. "I did."

She gazed down at the kitten in complete amazement. "D-did you just answer me?"

"Yes, I did," the kitten said, beginning

to purr faintly. "I am very grateful to you for rescuing me from that dangerous water trap. My name is Prince Flame. What is yours?"

"It's . . . it's just a normal fish tank," Rosie stammered, still hardly able to believe this was happening.

The kitten blinked up at her inquisitively with the brightest emerald eyes Rosie had ever seen, and she realized

that she hadn't answered his question.

"I'm Rosie Swales. Where did you come from? Did you say that you're *Prince* Flame?" The questions tumbled out of her.

"I come from a land far away. It is dangerous for me there. I need to hide here," Flame mewed.

"Is someone after you?" Rosie asked, feeling an instant rush of protectiveness.

Flame's bright eyes flashed with anger as he nodded. "My uncle Ebony. He has stolen the Lion Throne from me and rules in my place."

Rosie tried to take all this in. Flame's wet fur was sticking out around his cute pointed face like a spiky black halo. With his huge green eyes and triangular black nose, he was the most gorgeous kitten she had ever seen. "Aren't you a little small to be the ruler of a kingdom?" she asked gently.

"I will show you!" Flame squirmed and tried to wriggle out of the T-shirt.

Rosie quickly bent down so that he wouldn't have far to jump to the floor. Her eyes widened as she saw big glowing sparks begin to appear in Flame's long black fur. He bounded across the big room, and there was a bright, dazzling flash.

Rosie shielded her eyes, blinded for a second. She blinked hard, and when she could see again, she saw that the tiny kitten was gone, and standing in its place was a magnificent young white lion.

"Flame? Is that you?" Rosie gasped

nervously, eyeing the long teeth and sharp claws.

"Yes, Rosie. It is me. Do not be afraid," Flame answered in a deep velvety growl.

Before Rosie could get used to seeing the majestic young white lion, there was another bright flash, and Flame reappeared as a tiny, long-haired, coal-black kitten.

"Wow! I believe you about the Lion Throne now. That's an amazing disguise," Rosie said.

Flame began to tremble slightly. "It will not save me if my uncle's spies capture me. Will you help me to hide, Rosie?"

"Of course I will!" Rosie went over and bent down to stroke Flame's soft little ears. "You can live here with—" She stopped suddenly as she remembered that she was supposed to be finding new homes for her pets. "Oh. There's no way in the world that Mom and Dad are going to let me have *another* pet now," she said sadly.

Flame bowed his head. "I understand. Thank you for your kindness, Rosie. I will move on."

Tiny points of silver light began to glitter in Flame's long black fur, and his tiny form started to fade. Rosie felt a warm tingling sensation down her spine. It wasn't unpleasant, just a little strange.

"Don't go!" she burst out. "We'll figure something out. Maybe I could hide you or something!" She couldn't bear to think of Flame wandering

around all alone and helpless. Besides, she already felt fond of the adorable little kitten.

The sparks in Flame's black fur died away. "I would like to stay with you very much, Rosie," he mewed happily. "I will use my magic, so that only you will see and hear me when other humans are around."

"You can do that? That's amazing. There's no problem, then! Wait until I tell Jade about this. I bet she'll change her mind about pets being boring now!"

"No, Rosie. You cannot tell anyone about me. It must be our secret. Please, promise me." Flame's pointed face wore a serious expression.

Rosie hesitated. It was a shame she couldn't share her incredible secret with Jade, but if it would help to keep Flame safe, then she was happy to agree. "All right. It's just you and me."

"Thank you, Rosie," Flame purred.

Picking Flame up, Rosie carried him over to the bed and sat down with him. "You must be tired. Do you want to take a nap?"

Flame began purring contentedly as Rosie made a cozy nest for him in the quilt. "You know—I almost died when I saw you in the fish tank. I've heard of a catfish, but that was ridiculous!" she joked, smiling.

Flame's furry brow wrinkled, and he showed his sharp little teeth in a grin.

Rosie had forgotten that Daisy was stretched out relaxing in a fold of the quilt. The big rabbit lifted her head and her nose twitched. She got up and hopped over to say hello to the kitten.

Flame suddenly spotted Daisy. He let out a hiss, went rigid, and then shot behind Rosie's legs.

Rosie felt a laugh bubbling up inside her. "It's only Daisy, my pet rabbit," she sputtered. "She's really gentle. Come and meet her."

Flame didn't look convinced. His

bushy black tail was huge, and he
swished it from side to side nervously.
Very slowly, he crept out from behind
Rosie and gave Daisy a wary sniff.

Rosie watched closely, ready to
intervene if there was trouble. The
huge gray rabbit was at least ten times
the tiny kitten's size. If Daisy took a
dislike to Flame, she could give him
a painful bite. But Daisy gave a low,
friendly hum and half closed her
eyes, and Flame began to relax. A few
moments later he snuggled up against
Daisy's warm, furry side.

"There. I knew you'd be friends,"
Rosie said.

As she sat next to the rabbit and the
sleepy kitten, her worries about finding
new homes for her pets seemed to fade

for now. She had always loved animals and
knew lots about them, but never in her
wildest dreams had she expected to meet a
magic kitten!

Chapter
THREE

"I love having you living here with me!" Rosie said to Flame on Monday morning as she finished putting on her school uniform in her bedroom.

"I like it here, too. I feel safe with you," Flame purred. He was finishing the last mouthful of the sardines Rosie had smuggled from the kitchen.

There was a rustling noise from

Daisy's pen, where the rabbit was munching hay.

"I have to remember to put some more hay in for her before I leave," Rosie said.

Flame was licking his whiskers clean. "I can do that for Daisy," he mewed helpfully.

"Mmm? That's nice of you," Rosie

murmured, only half listening as she ran around searching for her schoolbooks and gym clothes. "Now, where's my schoolbag? Oh, there it is. I'm just going to the bathroom to brush my teeth, Flame. I'll be back soon."

A couple of minutes later, Rosie rinsed her toothbrush, put it back into the toothbrush holder, and came out of the bathroom. As she pushed her bedroom door, it seemed to snag on something that rustled loudly. Frowning, she pushed harder and managed to open the door just enough for her to edge into the room.

"Whoa! What's going on?" she gasped as she found herself pressed against a thick wall of hay.

A huge haystack filled the entire bedroom. The bed, furniture, pets, and Flame himself were all buried beneath it. Silver sparks were shooting up out of the hay in tiny puffs like smoke.

"Flame! What have you done?" Rosie scolded.

"I seem to have used too much magic to make Daisy's bed!" he replied in a muffled meow.

Mrs. Swales's voice floated up the stairs. "Rosie! Are you ready for school yet? Jade's here. I'll send her up!"

Rosie heard Jade's footsteps thudding up the stairs. "Do something, Flame," she whispered desperately.

Suddenly everything went into fast-forward.

Whoosh! A big fountain of silver sparks shot up toward the ceiling. *Rustle!* The haystack began to melt away and the lumpy shapes of the bed and furniture became visible. *Whisk!* Every last wispy bit of hay was sucked into Daisy's pen. And just in time—*flick!*— the hay arranged itself into a neat pile.

The last of the bright glittering sparks faded from Flame's black fur just as Jade stuck her head around the door.

There was a puzzled look on her face. "What's going on in here? I heard some *really* weird noises."

In a panic, Rosie glanced toward her bed, where Flame was sitting, calmly washing himself, but then she remembered that only she could see him. "I was . . . um, doing some exercises. Ready for school? Let's go," she said quickly, to avoid awkward explanations.

"You don't *do* exercises!" Jade said, grinning as she went back out.

"I do now!" Rosie called, shouldering her schoolbag. "See you later," she whispered over her shoulder to Flame. "You and Daisy have fun."

Flame just purred and began washing his ears.

Rosie and Jade sauntered down
the street. The trees in the gardens they
passed were already bursting with bright
green shoots. White flowers dotted the
bare soil.

"So, why didn't you come over
yesterday afternoon?" Jade asked.

Rosie frowned. What was Jade talking
about? Then, in a flash, she remembered.
She'd promised to go and play Jade's new
game after she finished her pet chores,
but in the excitement of finding Flame,
she had completely forgotten. "Oh, sorry.
I had more things to do than I thought,"
she said sheepishly.

"You don't need to make up excuses.
No one was forcing you to come or
anything," Jade said quietly.

Rosie felt awful. Jade was obviously

upset. "I was going to come, really, but then something happened . . ." She stopped, realizing that there was no way she could explain about Flame. "Look— why don't I come over tonight? We can work on our recycling project."

"I can't have anybody over while I'm doing homework," Jade said stiffly. "Mom says I mess around too much and never get anything done."

Rosie grinned. "She has a point!
We *do* play around a lot when we're
together!"

Jade's face relaxed and she gave a
short laugh. "I guess so."

"How about tomorrow after school,
then?" Rosie suggested. "No, wait.
That's no good, either. I'm going to
look at our new house with Mom and
Dad. Like I'm really looking forward
to that—*not!*"

"Why not?" Jade asked, and then a
worried look came over her face. "You're
not moving away, are you?"

Rosie shook her head. "No. The
house is just across town. I'm staying at
school and I'll still be able to see you
every day."

Jade punched the air and gave a

whoop. "Yay! That's fantastic, isn't it?
So what's the problem?"

Rosie put her hands on her hips.
"The problem is that the house is a tiny
dump, and my new bedroom's going
to be super small. You're not going to
believe this, but Mom and Dad said
I have to find new homes for all my
pets—apart from Daisy!"

Jade laughed with relief. "Is that
all? You'll be able to spend more time
with me when you don't have a
million boring animals to take care
of, won't you?"

Rosie gaped at her. "My pets aren't
old toys that I've outgrown, you know!
Why doesn't anyone seem to get that?
I bet you'd all be happier if I just threw
them in the garbage!"

"Hey, don't take it out on me!" Jade said.

"I'm not . . . ," Rosie said, still feeling rattled. "I just thought you'd understand. You *are* supposed to be my best friend!"

"I am—" Jade began.

"Well, it doesn't feel like it!" Rosie grumbled.

"Thanks for nothing!" Jade tossed her head. "Don't bother calling for me when you go to look at your stupid new house!" She stomped off down the street, her shoulder bag bouncing with every step.

Chapter
FOUR

Rosie sat at her usual desk right
at the back of the classroom. She was
glad that Jade's desk was two rows in
front, so she didn't have to face her again
just yet.

She still felt upset after their fight.
Maybe by recess they both would have
calmed down.

Rosie put her hand in her schoolbag

to take out her books and only just managed not to gasp aloud. There was something warm and furry inside! As she touched it, it began purring.

Oh no! Flame! What was he doing there?

Quickly checking that no one was watching, Rosie looked into her bag. Two mischievous green eyes glowed at her from the darkness.

"Flame!" she scolded gently. "Animals aren't allowed in school!"

"Do not worry. No one will know I'm here," he mewed.

Rosie wasn't too sure that it was a good idea to have Flame in class. It could lead to all kinds of problems, but it was too late now. Flame leaped out of her bag, walked boldly across a line of desks, and jumped up on top of a cabinet.

No one took any notice, and Rosie began to relax. Besides, having Flame close by was making her feel a lot better after arguing with Jade.

"Rosie Swales—are you listening?" a cheery voice called out.

Miss Brooks, her class teacher, had spiky blond hair. She always wore bright dangly earrings. Rosie really liked her.

Rosie blushed as she realized that Miss Brooks had been speaking to the class. "Sorry, Miss Brooks."

"You looked miles away. I hope it was somewhere nice," Miss Brooks said. She smiled as a ripple of laughter filled the room. "As I was saying, as part of our project on recycling, I'd like you all to think of unusual ways of reusing packaging."

Jade's hand shot up. "I've got one, Miss Brooks! My grandpa cuts plastic soda bottles in half to make mini greenhouses. He puts one over each lettuce, and it stops slugs from munching on them."

"What a great idea. Thanks for that, Jade. That's just the sort of thing I mean," Miss Brooks said. "So, get your thinking caps on, everyone." She beckoned to Rosie. "Could you come here, please?"

Rosie got up and went down to the front of the class.

There was a new girl sitting there, whom Rosie hadn't noticed earlier. The new girl had bronze-colored skin, and her black hair was braided in neat rows. She gave Rosie a nervous smile.

Rosie smiled back.

"Rosie, this is Uchena Nakuru. Will you work with her today and show her around?" said Miss Brooks.

"Sure. Hi, Uchena," Rosie said.

"Hi, Rosie," Uchena said shyly.

As Rosie and Uchena went back to Rosie's desk, they passed Jade. Rosie looked toward her friend, but Jade kept her head down.

"So do you have any ideas about what we can do with cardboard boxes?" Rosie said, once they were seated.

Uchena seemed to be thinking hard. "How about a really gigantic cardboard model of Disney World?"

"Yeah right!" Rosie said, going along with it. "Or a model of our school with little mini cardboard schoolkids and a mini

cardboard Miss Brooks!"

She and Uchena burst out laughing.

Rosie saw Jade look over to see what all the giggling was about. She could see that her friend looked miserable, and felt a pang of guilt for having so much fun with Uchena. But although she tried hard to stop laughing, Rosie's lips kept twitching.

Then she had a real idea. She told Uchena what it was.

"Yeah, that's cool," Uchena said when Rosie had finished explaining. "Let's do it."

After helping themselves to cardboard, scissors, and tape, Rosie and Uchena got to work.

Rosie had to remind herself not to keep glancing up at the cabinet where

Flame was dozing with his paws curled beneath him. By recess, the cardboard structure was really taking shape.

"All right, class, let's stop for recess," Miss Brooks called out. "You can continue with your projects afterward."

Everyone began filing out of the classroom. "I need to go to the bathroom. I'll see you outside," Uchena said.

"Do you want me to show you where it is?" Rosie asked helpfully.

Uchena shook her head. "It's okay. I'll find it."

Jade had hung back as the rest of the class left. She sauntered slowly over to Rosie's desk.

"What's that supposed to be?" She pointed at the lopsided cardboard

tower that Uchena and Rosie had been working on.

"It's a rat activity center for Midge and Podge," Rosie said.

"It's a pretty pathetic one if you ask me!" Jade scoffed.

Rosie usually would have seen the funny side and laughed along with her friend, but for some reason she found herself snapping, "Why do you care, anyway? It's just another pet thing!"

Jade's face darkened. She turned around to go, and her shoulder bag swung out in a wide arc. It swiped the activity center off the desk and onto the floor, where it broke apart into lots of small pieces.

Rosie gasped. "Look what you've done. That took us ages. You are so *mean*, Jade Ronson!"

Jade looked horrified. "I didn't mean to—" She took one look at Rosie's furious face. "Oh, what's the point?" she said disgustedly and marched out of the classroom.

Flame leaped down onto Rosie's desk. "I do not think Jade did that on purpose," he mewed softly.

"No. Neither do I," Rosie admitted in a small voice. "Jade's not like that. I don't know why I yelled at her. I'm just all mixed up right now."

She decided to stay in the classroom with Flame during recess. As she sat stroking his soft black fur, she felt herself calming down.

After about ten minutes, Flame jumped off her lap and onto the floor.

"I will fix that thing you are making, and then you will not be angry with Jade anymore," he mewed helpfully.

"I'm not sure you should do that," Rosie warned, remembering the hay disaster.

But it was too late. She could already feel the familiar prickling sensation down her spine.

Silver sparks ignited all over
Flame's long black fur, and his whiskers
crackled with electricity. He pointed
a tiny silky black paw at the bits of
battered cardboard, and a shower of
bright sparks shot out, swirling around
like a tiny snowstorm.

When the sparks cleared, Rosie
saw that an amazing rat-size cardboard
castle stood on the desk. "Wow! That's
so cool. It has windows and ramps

and even a tiny drawbridge. Midge and
Podge are going to love it!" she cried.

Rosie's classmates began drifting
back into the room as recess ended.

Uchena came straight over to Rosie.
She spotted the tiny castle right away.
"That's awesome! How did you finish it
so quickly?"

"I don't know. I wanted to get
an extra bit done and got carried
away . . . ," Rosie improvised as
everyone else began crowding around.

She saw Flame dart beneath the
desks, out of the way of all the legs and
feet. He trotted across the room and
then jumped up onto a windowsill.

"Look what Rosie did during recess,
Miss Brooks!" Uchena shouted as the
teacher came into the classroom. "She

finished the rat activity center. It's like something from a pet store!"

Miss Brooks came over to look at the castle. "Well done, Rosie. It's very good indeed."

"Uchena helped, too," Rosie murmured, going bright red. She didn't deserve all this praise, but there was no way she could tell anyone the truth. They'd never believe it, anyway. She left everyone still looking at the cardboard castle and started edging toward her seat.

But she almost ran into Jade, who was standing watching with her arms folded. "Jade! I wanted to say—" she began.

"Well, I don't how you could have fixed it so quickly, but everyone's really impressed with you now, especially

Uchena," Jade cut in. "I guess she's going to be your new best friend!"

"No! I like her, but—"

Jade had already turned and gone to sit near another schoolmate. As Rosie sat down, her heart sank. Somehow, and without even trying, she had managed to upset Jade again.

Chapter
FIVE

"Rosie! Hurry up and get in the car," called Mr. Swales. "The real estate agent's waiting for us at the new house."

Rosie walked across the front lawn at a snail's pace with Flame trotting invisibly at her heels. The horrible ordeal of going to look at the new house could not be put off any longer.

She got into the backseat, and Flame

jumped into her lap. As her dad drove across town, Rosie stared out the window, hardly noticing where they were going.

Ten silent minutes later, they turned onto Milton Street. Mr. Swales pulled up opposite a line of redbrick houses. The one on the end with a green door had a "Sold" sign stuck to the wall. Next to it, there was a big detached stone house with a front lawn and a fancy black iron gate.

"That's ours with the green door and the 'Sold' sign," Mrs. Swales said.

Rosie had figured that out for herself. *Why couldn't it be that big stone one next door, where all my pets could stay?* she thought.

Mrs. Swales saw where Rosie was

looking. "Mrs. Galloni, an Italian lady, lives
there. We met her when we first found the
house. She seems very nice."

A man in a suit was coming over.
Mr. and Mrs. Swales got out of the car
and shook hands with him. The real estate
agent unlocked the house, and Rosie
and Flame followed him and her parents
inside.

As she wandered through the downstairs rooms, Flame sniffed around, nosing into corners and looking at everything with his bright green eyes.

"What do you think of it? It's horrible, isn't it?" Rosie whispered to him.

He blinked up at her. "I think this house is a good, safe place."

"Really?" Rosie said, cheering up a tiny bit.

It must be okay if Flame liked it. Maybe living here wasn't going to be too bad, especially with Flame as her friend, and Daisy, too. If only there was some way she could keep *all* her pets.

Upstairs, the bathroom and bedrooms were neat and freshly painted. Rosie's new bedroom had bookshelves on the

white walls and a closet for her clothes.
From the window she could see into
Mrs. Galloni's backyard with its tall trees
and enormous garden shed.

Rosie's mom came and stood next
to her. "Well? What do you think? Do
you like your new bedroom?"

"It's all right. Except for it being the
size of a shoebox." In fact Rosie was
pleasantly surprised by how nice it was,
but she wasn't ready to say so. "I bet I
could squeeze Midge and Podge's cage
in here," she said casually.

"Don't start that again please,
Rosie," her mom warned.

"But I've hardly even said
anything—" Rosie began indignantly.

Her dad appeared in the doorway.
"Having a good talk, you two? Rosie,

your mom and I have a few things to discuss with the real estate agent. Do you want to wait in the car and read your book?"

Rosie nodded. Flame followed her as she went downstairs and out into the street. She was about to cross the road, when she spotted a large orange cat sitting on Mrs. Galloni's front step. It was wearing a bright blue velvet collar with a gold bell.

"Ooh, look, an orange tabby. Isn't he gorgeous? Let's go and say hello!"

Flame scampered after her as Rosie bent down to stroke the orange cat. "Hello there. I wonder what you're called. We're going to be neighbors," she said in a friendly voice.

Suddenly the front door opened and

a lady with curly dark hair and flashing
dark eyes stood there looking down
at her.

"Hey, you!" Mrs. Galloni shouted.
"Why are you back here? You are a
naughty girl. You should be ashamed
for throwing apple cores at Tinker.
Go now, before I call the police!"

"But, but I didn't . . . ," Rosie stammered, rising slowly to her feet.

"Go on, shoo! Shoo! Go find your nasty friends!" Mrs. Galloni bent down to sweep Tinker into her arms and slammed her door.

"Oh great. Our new neighbor thinks I'm some kind of pet tormentor!" Rosie fumed as she marched across the lawn and closed the front gate behind her. "Do you think I should go back and try to explain?"

Flame shook his head. "I think that lady is too angry to listen."

Rosie decided he was probably right. "Come on. Let's go and get in the car."

Once inside, Rosie felt too fed up to read. She sat there with Flame on her lap until her parents and the real estate agent came out of the house.

"Well, that's all taken care of," Mr. Swales said brightly as he settled in the driver's seat. He glanced at Rosie in the rearview mirror. "We'll be moving in about a month. Isn't that exciting?"

Rosie didn't answer. That meant she had four weeks to find homes for her pets.

*

Later that evening, Rosie opened the door to find Jade standing there. "Oh, uh . . . ," she murmured in surprise.

Jade smiled uncomfortably. "I bet I'm the last person you expected to see."

"Kind of." Rosie nodded. She smiled back. "I'm glad you're here, though. Do you want to come in?"

Jade looked relieved. "You bet!" She

stepped inside. "I came over to see if you're okay. My mom's been talking to your mom, who told her that she'd called the Pet Care Center. And I . . . um . . . I mean we . . . thought maybe *we* could give Midge and Podge a home."

"Really? But you don't even *like* animals!" Rosie said, amazed.

Jade shrugged. "That's because I've never been allowed to have pets. I'm sure I would like them if I gave myself the chance. How about if I look after Midge and Podge for a few days and see how it goes?"

"That's a wonderful idea!" Rosie said, grinning. "I can tell you all about rat behavior and how to care for them. And I've got a rat book you can borrow.

Rats are great pets, and they're really clean. Come up and see them!"

Jade followed her up to her bedroom.

Flame was lying snuggled up against Daisy, who was stretched out full-length on the rug, but of course Jade couldn't see him. The sight of the enormous rabbit and tiny kitten made Rosie smile. Maybe being friends with Daisy made

Flame feel less homesick for creatures from his own world.

"Wow! Look what Midge and Podge have done to their activity center!" Jade peered into the rats' cage at the cardboard castle, which now had frilly edges around the doors and windows. "Those rascals!"

Rosie grinned. "Behavior lesson number one. Rats nibble *everything*!"

She spent the next half hour telling Jade all about looking after Midge and Podge. ". . . I've got tons of food and bedding and stuff. You shouldn't need to buy anything for them for ages," she said finally.

"It's an awful lot to remember," Jade said, looking a bit worried.

"You'll get it soon. And I'll come

over if you get stuck," Rosie said breezily.
"So? When do you want me to bring
them over?"

For a moment, Rosie thought she
saw a nervous look pass briefly over Jade's
face, but then it was gone. "Now's good,"
her friend replied. "I'll take the food and
bedding if you carry the cage."

Delighted that Midge and Podge were
going to have a new home soon, and
even better, she'd still be able to see them,
Rosie pushed all doubts out of her mind.

She quickly got organized and then
trooped downstairs with Jade and went
next door. "I really should go and say
thanks to your parents. It's so nice of them
to let you have Midge and Podge," Rosie
said as she carried the cage into Jade's
kitchen.

"No, don't!" Jade said hastily.
"They're . . . er . . . playing cards with
my aunt and uncle. They get really
annoyed if I disturb them." She headed
for the stairs. "Let's go straight up to my
bedroom."

Rosie followed on tiptoe. Opening
her bedroom door, Jade dumped the
bags of bedding and food on the carpet

and then helped Rosie set everything up.

Rosie finally bent down to look in at Midge and Podge. "This is your new home, but I'll still see you lots and lots."

Midge and Podge looked out of their cage, their whiskers twitching excitedly as if they knew what she was saying. Rosie took a few sunflower seeds out of her jeans pocket and gave them some. "Be good little ratties for Jade, okay?" She turned to Jade. "Thanks a million for this."

"No problem," Jade said, grinning widely. "I'm just glad we're friends again."

"Me too. I'll leave you guys alone for now, and then call in the morning to see how you're doing. Bye for now," Rosie said.

As she went back into her house, she tried not to feel sad about Midge and Podge. It wasn't as if they'd be far away, and she was sure Jade was going to do her very best to be a good owner.

Chapter
SIX

Despite her good intentions, Rosie didn't sleep very well, worrying about how Midge and Podge were doing. It was hardly light when she woke the following morning. Across the room, Daisy was just a shadowy mound in her pen.

Rosie turned on her bedside light and then lay stroking Flame, who was

curled up against her pillow. "I'm so glad
you'll be coming with me and Daisy to
the new house," she said to him.

Flame purred and rolled over so she
could tickle his tummy. "I hope I can
do that, but if my uncle's spies find me,
I will have to leave suddenly."

"Maybe they'll never find you,
and then you can live with me always,"

Rosie said, determined to look on the bright side.

Flame's tiny face looked serious. "That is not possible, Rosie. One day I have to return and claim my throne."

Rosie nodded. She knew this was something she had to accept, but she didn't want to think about that just yet.

Suddenly a loud shriek rang out.

"What was that?" Rosie sat bolt upright, her heart racing.

Flame pricked up his ears. "I think it came from the house next door." He sprang onto the floor as Rosie threw back the quilt and flew over to the window.

Opening the window, Rosie leaned out. She could see that Jade's kitchen light was on.

There was another earsplitting shriek. "Eee-eek!" cried a woman's voice.

"It's Jade's mom! Come on, Flame!" Rosie rushed out of the bedroom without a second thought.

She hurtled downstairs in her bare feet, and went across the lawn and through the gate into the alleyway. As she ran into Jade's backyard, Flame tore after her, his silky black tail streaming behind him.

"Oh!" Rosie almost jumped out of her skin as a loud bark rang out. She heard strong claws scrabbling at the fence. She'd forgotten that a border collie lived next door to Jade.

Rosie quickly ran past the old garden shed outside Jade's kitchen. Suddenly the kitchen door burst open.

"Rosie! What are you doing here?"
Jade stood there in her pajamas.

"I heard screams. What's going on?"
Rosie said, peering around Jade.

Mrs. Ronson was perched on a stool
in the middle of the kitchen. "Help! Call
the exterminator!" she screamed.

"It's okay, Rosie. I'll handle it." Jade

turned back into the kitchen. "Mom, calm down!" she pleaded.

Suddenly two small brown-and-white shapes cannoned past Rosie and dashed into the garden. It was Midge and Podge.

"Hey, you two, come back!" Rosie called.

But the terrified rats weren't listening. To Rosie's horror, they ran toward the fence and wriggled under a small gap at the base of it.

"Oh no!" Rosie gasped. "That dog will get them!"

"Do not worry. I will save them!" Silver sparks flared in Flame's long black fur. He leaped onto Jade's fence, trailing a comet's tail of sparks behind him.

Rosie felt the warm magical tingling down her spine and heard a crackle of electricity. She clambered up onto the old garden shed to get a better look into Jade's neighbor's garden.

Midge and Podge were streaking across the lawn with the black-and-white collie snapping at their heels! Any second now, it was going to catch them!

Flame pointed a tiny black paw, and a fountain of colored sparks whooshed toward the dog. There was a blue flash. Where the collie had been, there was now a big, soft, fluffy ball, with two ears, four stubby legs, and a surprised-looking doggy face. As the dog ball rolled harmlessly across the lawn, Rosie gave a huge sigh of relief.

She looped one leg over Jade's fence and quickly dropped down the other side. Dashing over to Midge and Podge, she scooped them up and then ran out the back gate into the alleyway and came back through Jade's front gate.

She was only just in time. Lights were going on in some of the houses, and doors were opening. Rosie heard the collie barking and scrabbling at the fence again and knew that Flame's magic had worn off.

"Thanks so much for saving Midge and Podge," Rosie said to him.

"You are welcome," Flame purred, jumping down from the fence in a final burst of sparks.

Jade came out of the kitchen holding the rats' cage. "I went to get this. I thought you'd need it," she said in a subdued voice.

Rosie put the rats safely back into
their cage, before looking at Jade.
"Where's your mom?"

"Making some tea. She's okay now
that the rats are out of the house," Jade
told her.

"You didn't ask your parents if you
could have Midge and Podge, did you?"
Rosie guessed.

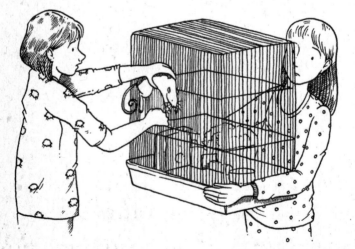

Jade shook her head, looking
downcast. "I knew they'd say no, but
I thought they'd get used to the idea
when they saw how well I looked after
them. But I must have not closed the
cage door properly, and Midge and
Podge got out. How was I supposed
to know Mom's terrified of rats and
mice? Yikes. I thought she was going
to scream the house down!"

"It's lucky Midge and Podge weren't
hurt. If Fla—I mean, if I hadn't jumped
over the fence and rescued them, they'd
be dog food by now!" Rosie said,
annoyed.

"I know. I'm really, really sorry," Jade
said in a small voice. "I . . . I wanted to
show you that I actually liked animals,
so you'd still want to be best friends

with me and not with Uchena."

Rosie saw tears glinting in Jade's eyes. She hesitated for only a moment before giving her a hug. "You'll always be my best friend, silly!" she said, starting to smile. "Your mom did look pretty funny standing on that chair!"

Jade gave a relieved laugh. "Yeah, she did!"

"I'd better take Midge and Podge back and then get dressed. Why don't you come by and get me before school?" Rosie said.

"See you soon then!" Jade beamed at Rosie and then waved at her as she went home.

Rosie didn't feel annoyed anymore as she put the rats' cage back onto its shelf, but she still felt sad. It was going to be up to the Pet Care Center to find Midge and Podge a new home. The rats' new owner could live anywhere and that meant she might never see them again.

Chapter
SEVEN

The following evening, Rosie and her parents had just finished dinner when the phone rang in the hall. Mr. Swales got up to answer it.

"Good news," he told Rosie, coming back into the kitchen. "That was the lady from the Pet Care Center. She might have someone willing to take your fish and stick bugs. She's also got someone who's interested in the gerbils, but so far no one's come forward for the rats or parakeets."

"Oh," Rosie said glumly, thinking that this was anything but good news. "It looks like my pets are all going to have to go to different homes."

"Well, it must be hard to find someone who wants to take care of many pets as you," her mom said reasonably.

"Exactly! That's why I should keep them!" Rosie said.

Her dad gave her a stern look. "Now, Rosie—you know very well that we've been through all this. And we *are* letting you keep Daisy."

Big deal, Rosie thought, but she was too sensible to say so. She jumped up from the table. "I'm going upstairs to read!"

When her parents weren't looking, she rubbed the tips of her fingers together to call Flame out from under the table. He trotted upstairs after her.

"Grrrr! I'm *so* fed up!" Rosie said, clenching her fists, when she and Flame were alone. "If we didn't have to move to a super tiny dollhouse, I could keep all my pets—" She stopped as an idea jumped into her head.

Flame twitched his ears and looked up at her. "What is it, Rosie?"

"I'm going to ask Gran if I can live with her! She's got a big spare room in her apartment. I don't know why I didn't think of it before. Come on, Flame. Let's go over there and ask her about it, right now."

"Perhaps you should tell your parents where you are going first?"

"No. They'll only try to talk me out of it," Rosie reasoned. "I want a chance to talk to Gran face-to-face. We can take the bus and be back before Mom and Dad even notice I'm gone. It'll be a fun adventure for us!"

Flame nodded, his bushy black tail sticking up perkily.

Rosie went and gave Daisy a quick

cuddle. "See you later. If this works, you won't have to be parted from all your friends," she told her as she stroked the rabbit's long velvety ears.

She put her sneakers on, grabbed her fleece jacket, and then held her shoulder bag open so that Flame could jump inside.

Rosie crept downstairs and went out, closing the front door quietly behind her. Holding the bag carefully so Flame wouldn't be jostled, she hurried to the bus stop at the end of the street.

But when she looked for her wallet to get the bus fare, it wasn't in her shoulder bag. "Oh no. It must be in my schoolbag. I can't risk going back to get it. We'll just have to walk. I think I can remember the way."

As she set off, Flame popped his
head up out of the bag and sniffed the
interesting smells.

Rosie walked quickly, passing the
familiar houses and stores. After about
fifteen minutes, she reached some streets
she didn't often walk down. "I think
that's where Mom goes to get her hair

done," she told Flame, pointing to a building.

After another twenty minutes, she came to a busy intersection. As she turned onto a long tree-lined street, she felt her heart sink. She didn't remember ever coming here before, and she didn't recognize any of the names of the side streets.

Rosie's feet were starting to ache now, and she felt hot and sweaty. There was no one around to ask for directions.

Flame reached up out of the bag and patted her arm with a tiny front paw. He gave a mew of sympathy. "Are you all right, Rosie?"

"Not really. I'm tired and thirsty, and I think we're completely lost," she said, starting to feel tearful.

A large orange cat with a bright blue velvet collar and a gold bell came running out of a side street. Something about it seemed very familiar.

"Hey! That's Tinker. What's he doing way over here? He belongs to Mrs. Galloni, our new neighbor!" Rosie said.

Flame frowned. "Maybe it is you and I who are close to Mrs. Galloni's house?"

Rosie caught sight of the nearby street sign. It read "Milton Street." Flame was right! Despite getting lost, they had somehow found their way across town and ended up almost at her new house!

"So we're nowhere near Gran's apartment. What a waste of time," Rosie moaned.

She saw Tinker amble into the middle of the road and sit down to wash himself. "Look at that silly cat. He'll get run over if he's not careful. Tinker! Come here," she called out.

Tinker yawned and blinked, but didn't move.

Rosie watched as Flame leaped into the road, obviously intending to attract Tinker's attention. But just as Flame trotted up to him, the orange cat got up and ambled to the other side of the road.

An enormous truck rounded the

corner and began hurtling straight toward Flame. Rosie's heart missed a beat. The driver hadn't seen the tiny black kitten against the dark road! Flame started to run, but he wasn't going to be able to get out of the way in time. Without a second thought, Rosie dashed into the road and grabbed Flame.

Holding him in her arms, she leaped for the sidewalk, but headlights blinded her, and there was a loud squeal of brakes as the truck skidded toward her.

Everything seemed to happen in slow motion.

An explosion of bright sparks burst out all around Rosie, and she felt a familiar tingling down her spine. Her whole body seemed to ripple. There was a strange collapsing sensation, like the air

going out of a balloon. Wind whistled
past Rosie's ears, and the road seemed
to rush up to meet her.

Flame had shrunk them both to
the size of mice!

Rosie crouched there as the
mountainous truck roared overhead,
with a thunderous noise that made
the road shake. The second it had gone,
Rosie hurtled to safety, her miniature
legs feeling numb.

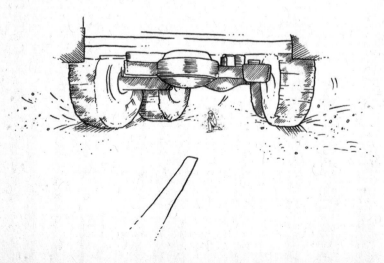

Moments later, Rosie came up against a curb as tall as a stone wall. She turned around to see that the truck driver was standing in the road, scratching his head. A few moments later, he climbed back into the truck and drove away.

"Phew! That was *way* too close!" Rosie turned back and stepped onto the curb.

She was normal size again!

Flame looked up at her, his emerald eyes bright. "You were very brave to risk yourself to save me. Thank you, Rosie," he purred gratefully.

Rosie kissed the top of his fluffy jet-black head. "I wasn't really. I just couldn't bear it if anything happened to you. Besides, you ended up saving us *both* with your magic!"

Rosie saw Tinker strolling back into the street. "That silly cat has no road sense. I think we'd better take him home, before he gets into trouble," she decided.

Flame mewed in agreement. Rosie put him down, picked up Tinker, and tucked him under one arm. Flame trotted along at her ankles as she turned onto Milton Street. But Rosie's steps gradually slowed as she remembered how unfriendly Mrs. Galloni had been the first time they'd met.

"I don't want to get shouted at again. I'm just going to knock on the door, hand Tinker over, and run for it," she said to Flame.

Chapter
EIGHT

Mrs. Galloni opened the door at
once, giving Rosie no time to even catch
her breath. Her face broke into a huge
smile. "You have found Tinker! I keep
him in at night, but the naughty boy
ran outside when I was bringing in my
laundry! Thank you so much for bringing
him home. Come in, my dear. What's
your name?"

"Rosie. Rosie Swales. I'm going to be living next door to you," Rosie said a bit warily.

"Ah, yes, I remember now," Mrs. Galloni said, her dark eyes sparkling. "I made a mistake the last time we met. I thought you were a bad girl, and I was rude."

Rosie put Tinker down and he ran straight into the house.

Rosie hesitated on the doorstep with Flame invisible at her heels, but then found herself swept into a large bright kitchen. It had yellow walls and a big sideboard with lots of blue-and-white plates and mugs. There was a wildlife calendar pinned to one wall next to a poster of a polar bear.

"I owe you an apology, Rosie,"

Mrs. Galloni said, stroking Tinker, who
was rubbing himself against her legs.
"I can see you love animals, like me.
I am a very silly lady, but I can make
it up to you, can't I?"

"That's okay," Rosie said. She felt
herself going a bit pink. "You don't have
to."

But Mrs. Galloni insisted that she sit
down at the kitchen table. "I can make

you a banana milkshake. Do you like chocolate cake, too? I made one this morning."

Rosie's tummy rumbled. It seemed like a long time since dinner and the long walk had made her hungry. "Okay, thank you very much."

She put her shoulder bag down. As Mrs. Galloni moved around her kitchen, Flame sat next to Rosie's ankles.

Mrs. Galloni brought over the milkshake and cake and then sat down opposite Rosie. "It is lucky for me that you and your parents are at your new house this evening or you would not have seen Tinker. I expect you're getting ready to move in."

"We're not at the new house. I'm here all by myself," Rosie said around a mouthful of the delicious cake.

"Oh. Why is that? Your mama, she tell me that you live across town," Mrs. Galloni said, looking puzzled.

"I didn't mean to come here. I'd planned to catch a bus over to my Gran's, but I forgot my wallet and so I had to walk," Rosie told her. "But I got lost and ended up coming here by mistake. And that's how I saw Tinker in the road . . ." Rosie gulped. Suddenly all the worries of the past two weeks seemed to flood over her.

"Oh dear. What is the matter?" Mrs. Galloni asked kindly, looking closely at Rosie. "You can tell me."

"It's just that . . . ," Rosie began, biting her lip, and then it all came bursting out. She told Mrs. Galloni

everything. "And I just can't bear it . . ."
As Rosie finished explaining, tears began
trickling down her face.

"I think I understand." Mrs. Galloni
reached for a box of tissues and handed
one to Rosie. "Tell me, darling, do your
mama and papa know where you are?"

"No. I didn't think I'd be this long,
so I didn't leave a note . . ." Rosie
sniffled.

Mrs. Galloni patted her arm gently. "What is your phone number? I will call your parents to tell them you are safe. Then you and I will have a long talk. I think I may be able to help you," she said mysteriously.

Rosie didn't see how anyone could help her, but as Mrs. Galloni went to call her parents, she started to feel better. "She's really nice once you get to know her, isn't she?" she whispered to Flame.

Flame nodded. "I like her. I think she will be a good friend."

Left alone in the quiet kitchen with Flame, Rosie gradually became aware of faint noises drifting in through the open door. Her chin came up as she strained to hear them. There were tiny squeaks, whistles, and contented little chatters.

What could it be?

She was really tempted to go and have a look. "Do you think Mrs. Galloni would mind if I went into her living room?" she asked Flame, getting up from her chair and wandering across the kitchen.

There was no answer.

Rosie turned around. Flame seemed to have disappeared. She came back and looked under her chair and then knelt down to peer under the table, but there was no sign of the tiny black kitten.

"Flame? Where are you?" she said, beginning to feel worried.

She had a sudden thought. Picking up her shoulder bag, she slipped her

hand inside. "Ah, *there* you are . . ."
Rosie's fingers brushed against a tightly
curled furry little bundle.

Then she realized that Flame was
trembling all over, and his heartbeat
fluttered against her fingers. Rosie felt
a stir of alarm as she opened the bag
wider. A pair of troubled green eyes
glowed at her from the dark interior.

"What's wrong? Are you sick?" she
asked gently.

"My uncle's spies are very close,"
Flame whined in terror.

Rosie bit back a gasp. The moment she
had been hoping would never come was
here. Flame was in terrible danger. Even
though she hated to think of losing her
friend, she knew she was going to have to
be strong.

"Are . . . are you leaving right now?"
she asked.

Flame shook his head. "I will stay
inside here. My enemies may pass me by,
and then I will be able to stay."

"Right! We're leaving! I'll think of
somewhere to hide you—" Rosie decided.

"No, Rosie. It is no use," Flame
interrupted. "Just leave me for a little
while." Flattening his ears, the tiny kitten
curled into an even tighter ball.

"All right." Rosie stood up. She tucked the bag under Mrs. Galloni's kitchen chair and then moved away. There was nothing she could do except cross her fingers and toes, and hope like crazy that Flame's enemies wouldn't find him.

Chapter
NINE

"I have spoken to your parents, Rosie. They were very worried about you, but are relieved to know that you are safe with me. They're going to drive over and pick you up. I have something to show you while we're waiting for them. Come with me."

Rosie hardly heard Mrs. Galloni, she was so worried about Flame, but she

followed her through the living room
and into a sunroom.

It was a large light room, with bright
rugs and comfortable seats. As Rosie
looked around, she gasped. There were
cages, pens, and glass tanks all neatly
arranged on wooden shelves. She could
see pet mice, guinea pigs, and different
breeds of dwarf rabbits. There were
brightly colored fish in the tanks, and
even what looked like a small snake in
one of them.

Despite herself, Rosie's eyes grew
round with amazement.

"Well. What do you think?"
Mrs. Galloni asked.

"It's . . . fantastic. Like animal
heaven . . . ," Rosie gabbled, hardly able
to take it in.

"Good evening!" shrieked a hoarse voice.

"Oh!" Rosie spotted a large upright cage behind a potted fern. Inside there was a handsome green-and-blue parrot, with a bright red crest.

"That's Rufus. I've had him for a long time," Mrs. Galloni said proudly. "He loves to talk."

"Pieces of cake! Pieces of cake!" Rufus shrieked.

"Hello, Rufus. Aren't you gorgeous?" Rosie said, her eyes shining. She turned back to Mrs. Galloni. "Do you run a pet rescue center or something?"

Mrs. Galloni smiled. "Not exactly. I just love animals. These are all my pets. They are like my family. If people

ask me to take care of a pet or give it a
home, I can never say no."

Just like me, Rosie thought.

"I have so many pets now, it's a big
job to look after them all," Mrs. Galloni
said.

Rosie nodded. "My best friend, Jade,
is always complaining because I spend

more time with my pets than with her."

Mrs. Galloni's curly dark hair wobbled as she nodded. "My friends say that to me, too!"

Rosie smiled.

"I have a wonderful idea," Mrs. Galloni said thoughtfully. "I have lots of space, as you can see. Would you like to bring your pets to live in my house?"

Rosie thought she might have to pinch herself to see if she was dreaming. "You'd really have them all in here?"

"Certainly, but there are some conditions," Mrs. Galloni said.

Rosie didn't care what they were. She felt like she'd agree to almost anything.

"Although your pets can live here, they would still belong to you, so you would have to buy their food and bedding, and come over every day to look after them," Mrs. Galloni explained. "And in return, you would help me to look after my pets."

Rosie thought the idea was fantastic! "It would be kind of like a pet hotel, wouldn't it?"

Mrs. Galloni smiled. "Yes. A pet hotel. What do you say?"

Rosie didn't need to think twice.
She could keep *all* her pets, and she'd get
to spend time with even more animals.
She couldn't wait to make friends with
Mrs. Galloni's pets, especially Rufus
the parrot. "I say, yes please, times ten!
Thank you so, so much! I can't wait to
tell Mom and Dad. Now I actually *want*
to move!"

Mrs. Galloni smiled delightedly.
"Then it is settled. I'll leave you here
to have a good look around. I'm going
to boil the kettle for tea. Your parents
should be here soon."

"Okay." Rosie wandered around the
sunroom, feeling as if she were walking
on air.

Midge, Podge, her gerbils, stick bugs,
and fish were all going to love it in here.

Daisy would live next door, with her and Flame . . .

Flame!

Rosie's tummy gave a lurch as she dashed back into the kitchen. She grabbed her bag while Mrs. Galloni's back was turned, and ran back into the living room with it.

Her fingers shook as she opened the bag and looked inside. It was empty.

Had Flame's enemies found him? Maybe they'd dragged him away to his home world, or worse.

"Oh no! Flame? Where are you?" Rosie whispered urgently, feeling really scared for him.

There was a bright white flash and a crackle of sparks from the sunroom.

Rosie ran inside, her heart pounding.

On the rug stood a magnificent young white lion. Silver sparks glittered in his fur like thousands of tiny diamonds.

Prince Flame! He was no longer in disguise as a silky black kitten. Rosie gasped. She had almost forgotten how stunning he was in his true form.

An older-looking gray lion with a kind, wise face stood next to Prince

Flame. And then Rosie knew that Flame was leaving for good.

"Oh, Flame. I'm really going to miss you," Rosie said, her voice breaking.

Prince Flame smiled sadly. "I will miss you, too. You have been a good friend, but now I must go. My enemies are very close."

Rosie blinked away tears. She stretched out her hand. Prince Flame lowered his regal head and allowed her to stroke him one last time before he backed away.

"Be well. Be strong, Rosie," he said in a deep velvety roar.

Rosie waved as both big cats began to fade. There was a final spurt of silvery sparks that sprinkled down around Rosie, and then they were gone.

"Take care, wherever you go, Prince Flame," she murmured.

"Rosie!" called her mom's voice.

Rosie took a deep breath. She would never forget her wonderful friendship with the magic kitten.

As she turned to go to her parents, she felt a smile breaking out on her face. "Coming, Mom. I've got some amazing news!"

About the Author

Sue Bentley's books for children often include animals or fairies. She lives in Northampton, England, and enjoys reading, going to the movies, and sitting watching the frogs and newts in her garden pond. If she hadn't been a writer, she would probably have been a skydiver or brain surgeon. The main reason she writes is that she can drink pots and pots of tea while she's typing. She has met and owned many cats, and each one has brought a special sort of magic to her life.

Don't miss these Magic Kitten books!

Don't miss these Magic Ponies books!

Don't miss these Magic Puppy books!

Don't miss these Magic Bunny books!